The Underbed

The Underbed
Copyright © 1990 by Good Books, Intercourse, PA
17534
International Standard Book Number: 0-934672-79-2
Library of Congress Catalog Card Number: 89-28884
All rights reserved. Printed in the United States of
America. No part of this book may be reproduced in
any form or by any means, electronic or mechanical,
including photocopying, recording or by information
storage and retrieval system, without permission.

Library of Congress Cataloging-in-Publication Data
Hoellwarth, Cathryn Clinton. 1957–
    The underbed / by Cathryn Clinton
Hoellwarth; illustrated by Sibyl Graber Gerig.
        p. cm.
    Summary: Tucker's mother helps him get rid of
the monster that stays under his bed, explaining
she had the very same trouble when she was little.
    ISBN 0-934672-79-2: $12.95
    [1. Fear—Fiction. 2. Bedtime—Fiction.] I.
Gerig, Sibyl Graber, ill. II. Title.
PZ7.H67125Un   1990
[E]—dc20   89-28884

The Underbed

Good✿Books®

Intercourse, Pennsylvania 17534

It was dark. Tucker lay in the middle of his bed, but he couldn't stand it any longer. He was scared. He leaped out of bed and ran into the living room.

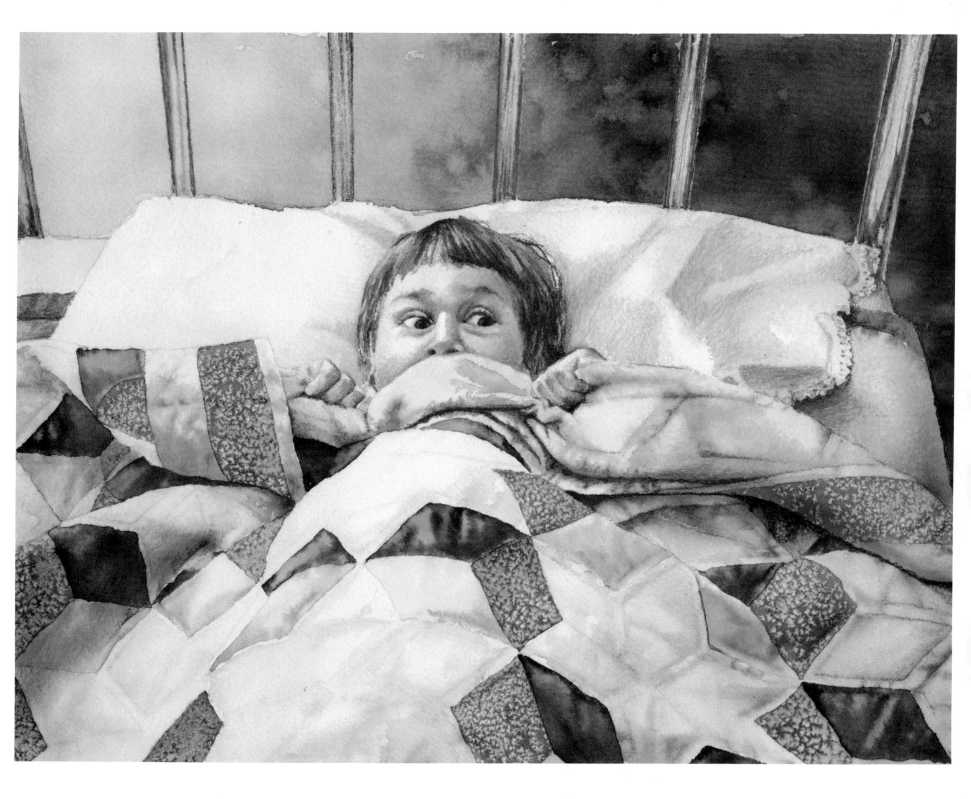

His mother was sitting in her favorite chair reading a big, fat book. He jumped right onto her lap and said, "I'm afraid."

"Of what?" his mother asked.

"The Underbed," he answered.

"Oh yes," his mother said, "I have heard of Underbeds."

"Does it live under your bed?" she asked.

"Uh-hmm," Tucker said, "and it has squishy octopus arms that grab at your legs if you stand too close to the bed."

"How do you get in bed then?"

"I run and jump as far as I can to get right in the middle of the bed. It can't get me there."

"Oh," said his mom, "I see."

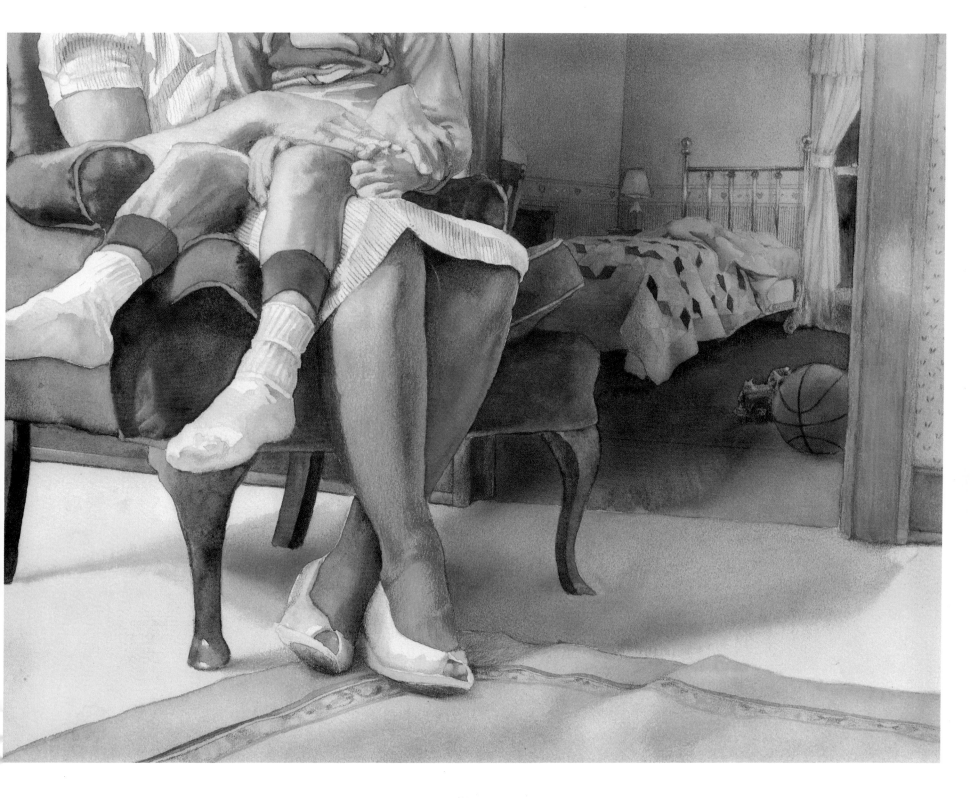

"Can you tell me more about it, Tucker?"

"It has orange googly eyes that glow in the dark."

"Just what I thought," his mother said. "It sounds like the one that lived under my bed when I was little."

"For real, Mom?"

"He was just as real as yours is, Tucker."

"What did you do, Mom?" Tucker asked.

"I told your gramma about it, and we got rid of it."

"You did? How?"

"Well," she paused and thought for a moment. "First, Gramma told me that Underbeds can't stand the light."

"Are you sure, Mom?" Tucker asked.

"Yep," she said. "Just think about the sun."

"Every morning the sun comes up ready for work. It brings light, and chases away the night. Then we have a new day. When you shine the light on the Underbed it has to leave. Just like the night."

"What did you do, Mommy?"

"Your gramma got a bright flashlight, threw back the covers and shined the light under the bed. I was so scared my knees wobbled like wet noodles, but I got down and looked under the bed. Sure enough, it was gone." She snapped her fingers and said, "Just like that."

"Did it stay away for good?" Tucker asked.

"Oh yes," she answered. "Once an Underbed sees that you know how light works, he won't even try to come back."

"Mommy, could we do that too?"

"Sure, Tucker." She gave him a quick squeeze.

"I'll go get our big red flashlight, the one we use for camping. That should take care of it." His mom left.

"I'll get my baseball bat," Tucker said. "Just in case."

They met outside Tucker's room. Tucker's mom tiptoed toward the bed. Tucker stayed right behind her.

"Ready?" she whispered. Tucker nodded. His mom got real close to the bed. "First, I will count to three, then I will throw back the covers and flash the light. Got it?" Tucker nodded again.

"One, two, three."

She whipped back the covers and quickly shined the light under the bed. Nothing moved, including Tucker. His mom slowly bent down and looked under the bed.

"All clear," she said with a smile.

"He's gone. He can't come back. Come, look for yourself."

Tucker walked forward. He peeked under the bed. There was nothing there.

"We got it," he shouted.

His mom gave him a whopping bear hug and said, "I couldn't have done it without you." She tucked him into bed and kissed him goodnight.

For the next three nights Tucker and Mom checked under his bed, but nothing was there. That old Underbed was gone for sure.

Tucker's mom said he could stop his jumping into the middle of the bed now, but Tucker didn't miss a night. He even added spins and somersaults to his flying leaps!